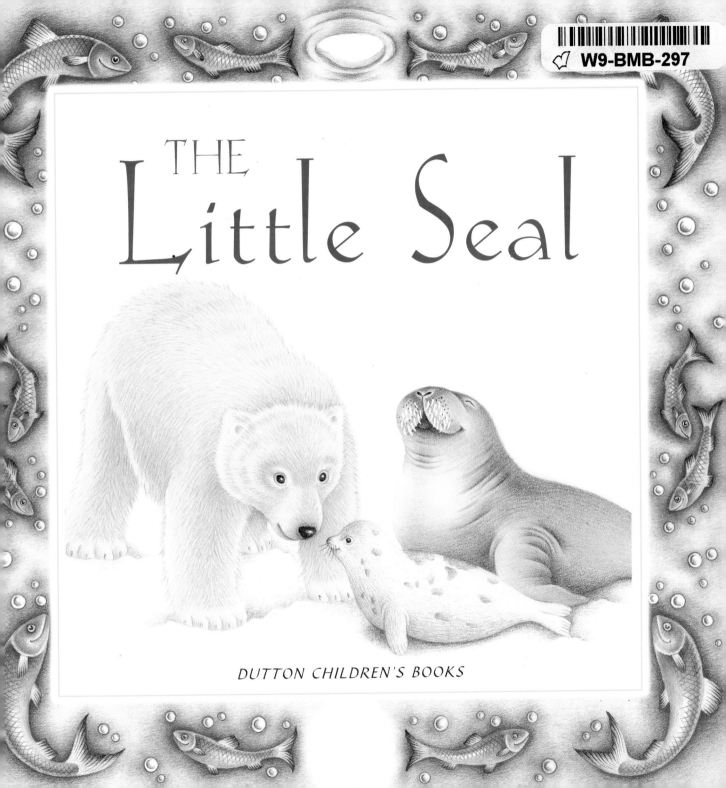

THE Little Seal

DUTTON CHILDREN'S BOOKS

In a faraway land, covered in sparkling ice and snow, a baby seal nestled against his mother's warm fur. The seal pup was soft and fluffy, the most beautiful thing his mother had ever seen. "I will call you Nuka," she said.

Soon, Nuka began exploring his icy home. He liked to watch the seabirds swirling high in the sky. He played and romped with his two best friends—Sesi, a stout young walrus, and Miki, a fuzzy polar bear cub. With Nuka in the lead, mischief was never far away.

One day, Miki, the polar bear cub, asked, "Nuka, what's happening to your fur?"

Nuka looked at his reflection in the sea. His white baby fur was changing. In its place short, gray fur was growing. "I'm getting my grown-up fur," he said proudly. **"I'm getting big and strong!"**

Nuka's mother heard and said, "That's a good thing, little one. You'll need to be strong for the journey ahead."

"What journey?" asked the little seal, looking worried.
"Where are we going?"

His mother explained that the seasons were changing.
It was time for the seal herd to move to their summer home.
"It will be a great adventure," she said. "We will swim
farther than you have ever dreamed."

"But I like having adventures with Miki and Sesi,"
grumbled Nuka. "I want to stay here."

His mother shook her head.
"I'm sorry, little one, but your place is with the herd."

The next day, as the ice sparkled in the early-morning sun, the seals gathered at the edge of the ocean. All were excited by the journey ahead—all except Nuka.

The little seal was frightened and sad. He didn't want to leave his home and friends. "Good-bye, Nuka!" cried Miki and Sesi. "We won't forget you!" Nuka waved good-bye, then slipped into the dark, chilly water.

As the herd swam farther and farther into the deep ocean, the little seal missed his playmates terribly. He longed to return to the home he knew. "I won't have any friends at this new place," the little seal said quietly. "I don't want to go!"

And so, while his mother wasn't looking, Nuka slipped away from the others and **headed for home**.

The little seal swam and swam. "I must be nearly home," he said to himself. "Imagine how surprised Miki and Sesi will be to see me!"

He paddled to the surface to see where he was.

When Nuka poked his head out of the water, he could see no sign of the familiar shore. He was all alone in the cold, vast ocean. And he was lost!

"Mother!" the little seal cried, suddenly afraid. "Where are you?"

A huge **splash** made Nuka jump. He thought it must be the herd, so he swam toward the noise as fast as his flippers would carry him. "Mother!" he called. "Wait for me!"

But it was not the seal herd. Instead, Nuka came face-to-face with a very big, very grumpy-looking whale.

Summoning all his courage, the little seal spoke up. "Excuse me, Mr. Whale, have you seen my seal herd swim by?"

"No!" boomed the whale. "Now leave me alone. I am busy!"

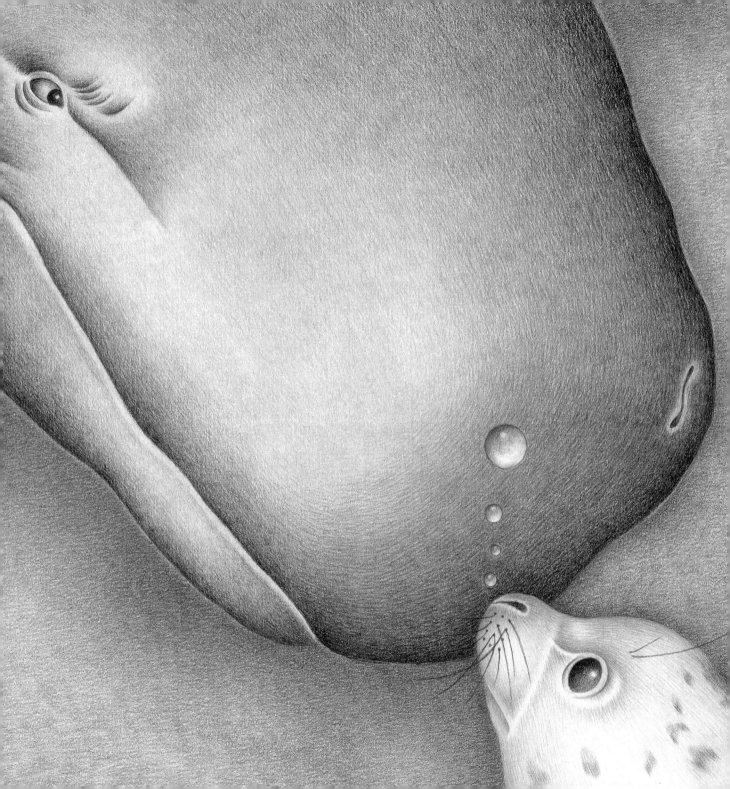

Well, Nuka was so upset that he forgot to be afraid. "I think you're mean not to help me!" he blurted. "You can't have many friends—you're much too rude."

"You're right," said the whale, surprised at the little seal's bravery. "I don't have many friends. Everyone is scared of me because I'm **so big.** That makes me sad. And very grumpy, too." The big whale sighed.

"I'm not scared of you," Nuka said, smiling shyly. "And I really need a friend. Could you help me find my herd?"

The whale's dark eyes opened wide, and his enormous mouth curved into a smile.

"Yes, I'll help you. My name is Atka. What's yours?"

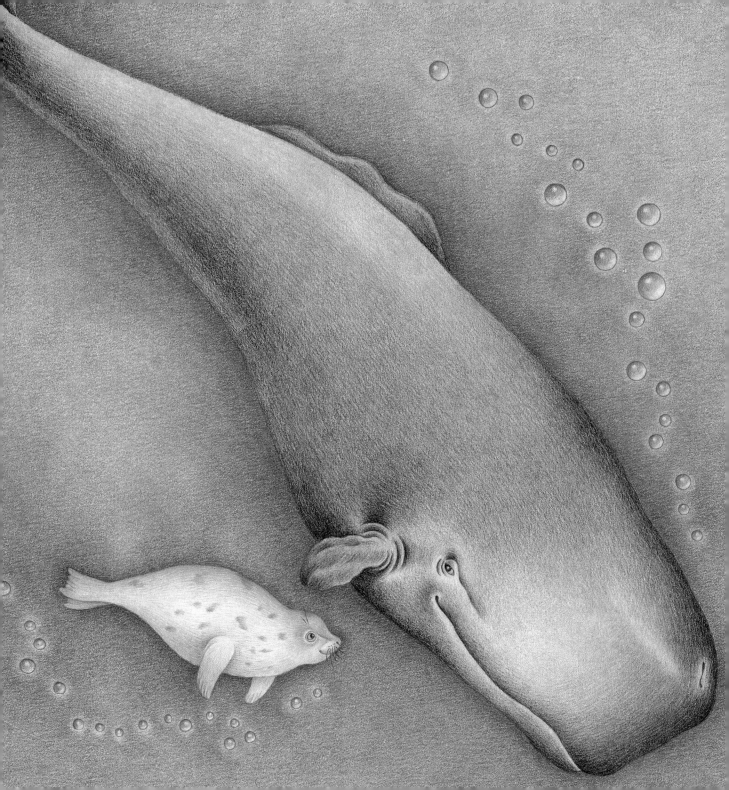

The little seal and the big whale set off through the chilly waters.
Before long, Atka said, "Let's swim to the surface to see if we can
spot your herd."

Sure enough, there was a group of seals on the icy shore.
"It's the herd—my herd!" he cried in delight.

His mother rushed to her little one. "Nuka! Where have you been?
I was so worried!" she said, and folded the happy pup into
a warm hug. The little seal was home at last.

"I've been making new friends," he said,
smiling at Atka.

By the end of his journey, the little seal had more friends than ever. Now, wherever he goes, Nuka is sure that fun and adventure await.

And when he must say good-bye, the little seal isn't sad. For he knows that even when they are apart, his friends are always with him —in his heart.

For Matthew – S.H.
For Nicole & Ashley – S.B.

Copyright © 2007 by The Templar Company plc

Published in the United States in 2007 by Dutton Children's Books,
a division of Penguin Young Readers Group
345 Hudson Street, New York, New York 10014
www.penguin.com/youngreaders

First published in the UK in 2007 by Templar Publishing,
an imprint of The Templar Company plc

Designed by Caroline Reeves

Printed in Malaysia

First American Edition

ISBN: 978-0-525-47839-3

2 4 6 8 10 9 7 5 3 1